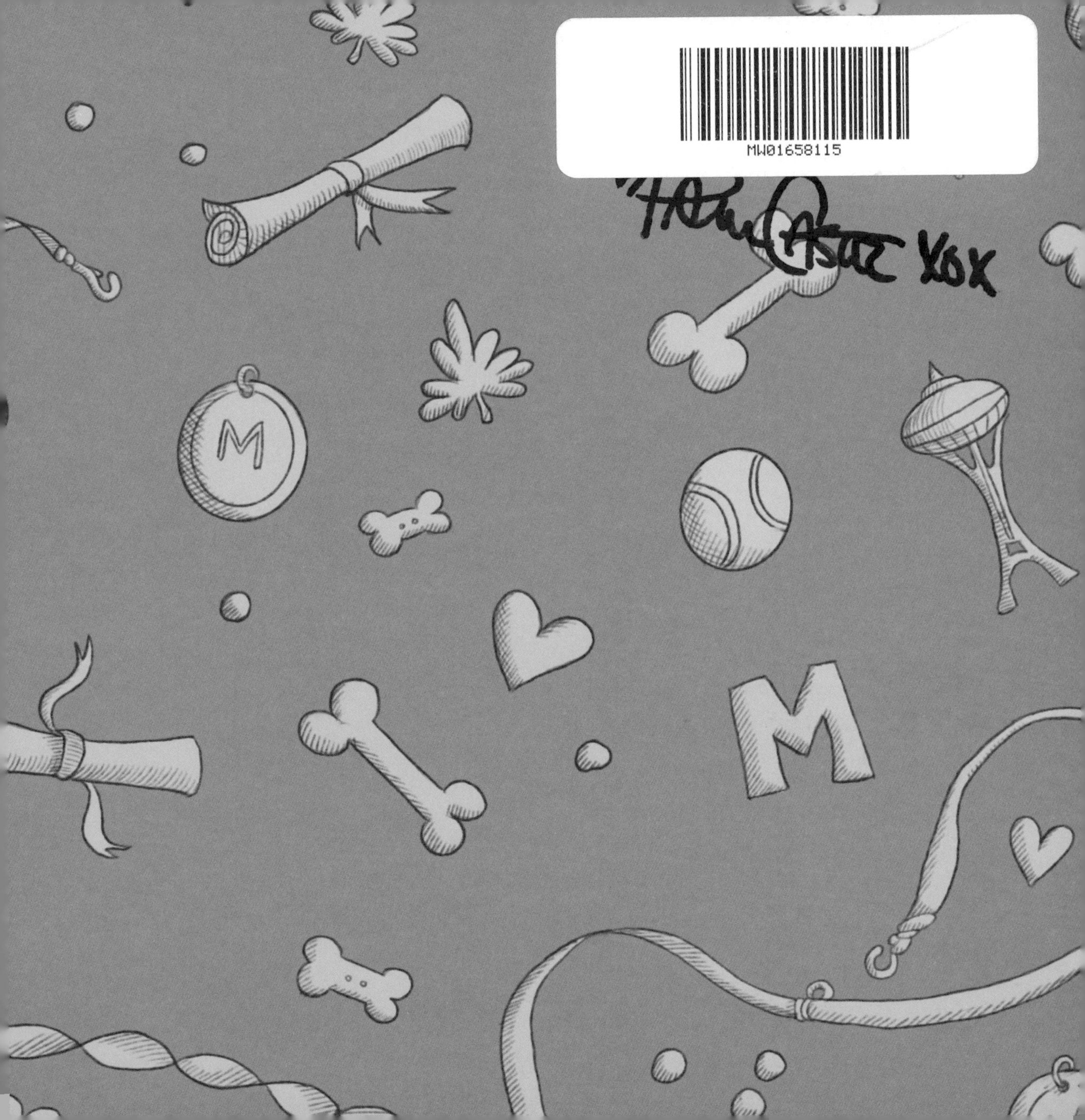

MR MAPLE

A GUIDE DOG'S JOURNEY

PAUL CASTLE

Published by Paul Castle Studio
PaulCastleStudio.com
First Printing
Design and Layout by Matthew Castle
ISBN: 979-8-9891871-2-6

FOR MAJOR,
MARATHON, MIKEY,
MASCOT, MATRIX,
MURDOCK, MADRID,
& MAPLE

Introduction

Long before they find their perfect match, guide dogs begin an extraordinary journey. Mr. Maple and his 7 brothers were born at Guide Dogs for the Blind, where they received early care, cuddles, and gentle handling. From the very start, they were loved.

At around 8 weeks old, puppies like Mr. Maple travel to live with volunteer Puppy Raisers, who teach them basic skills, house manners, and (most importantly) confidence and kindness. These first families help shape a well-rounded pup, preparing them for a future career in service.

When the puppies are around 14–18 months old, they return to GDB for formal training with professional instructors. Over several months, they learn to avoid obstacles, stop at curbs, navigate crowds, and make smart

decisions—even if it means disobeying a command to keep their handler safe.

From there, each dog chooses their own path. Some become guide dogs, while others go on to serve in different roles—like helping veterans, comforting patients, or assisting children. And some simply decide their calling is to be a much-loved pet.

If they choose a life of guiding, dogs like Mr. Maple are carefully matched with a person who is blind or visually impaired. This partnership is built on trust, teamwork, and love—and it changes both lives forever. Eventually, every guide dog retires, but it's far from the end of their journey. Guide dogs like Mr. Maple will remain as (very spoiled) family pets, while their blind handlers prepare to work with a new guide dog.

Now, come along and follow the paws of a very special pup, as he takes each step on his way to becoming...
Mr. Maple, the Guide Dog!

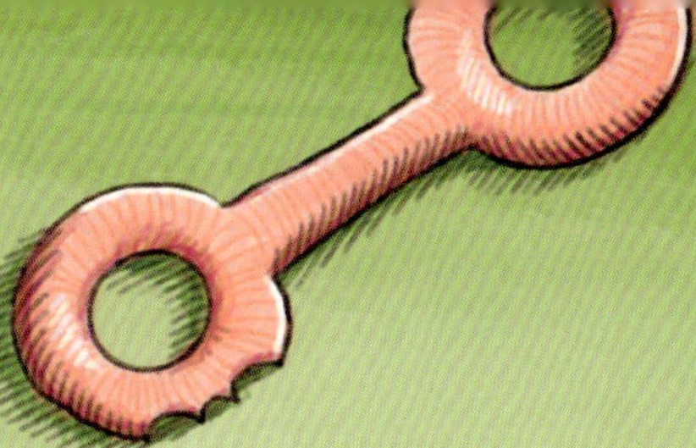

A litter of puppies, some black and some yellow,
Enter the world, all happy and mellow.
With tiny paws and soft snoring snoozes,
Each puppy embarks on the life that he chooses!
Some will be guide dogs and others will not,
But each of them give it their very best shot.
Snuggly and sweet, yet daring and bold,
Mr. Maple's story is soon to unfold...

The Puppy Truck

Oh look! Here it comes! A puppy-filled truck!
Delivering puppies and wishing them luck!
Mr. Maple arrives at a home filled with heart,
A place he will learn to get a head start.
They'll teach him to love, to cuddle, and grow,
And do all the things he doesn't yet know.
Gaining the skills that all Raisers bring,
A puppy in training—what a
wonderful thing!

HOW TO
TAKE THE LEAD

Eager to learn, Mr. Maple is bright.
Obeying commands and doing what's right.
He's not always perfect, but never gives up,
On his quest to become the puppiest pup!
As time passes by, his tail grows longer,
Mr. Maple gets bigger, and braver, and stronger.
And when he's full-grown, a bittersweet day,
He'll say his farewells and be on his way...

PHASE 1
OBSTACLE COURSE
PHASE 2
DISTRACTION ROUTES
PHASE 3
OBEDIENCE
CHOOSE
YOUR OWN
PATH
NO BARKING

He did it! He made it! The first day of class!
There isn't a test Mr. Maple can't pass.
One at a time, he sails through the phases.
The harder they get, the more he amazes.
Led by instructors who handle with care,
He meets every challenge with skills that are rare.
Calm on the outside, but shouting inside:
"I'm going to do it! I'm going to GUIDE!"

The time has arrived, the path has been laid.
Dear Mr. Maple, your match has been made!
Your purpose in life has brought you this far,
An answer to prayers and a wish on a star.
Your person is waiting, a cane in their hand,
Preparing to start an adventure so grand.
They may not see faces or signs on the street,
But you'll be their eyes, their courage, their feet.

GUID

"Can't see? No worries, I'll be your eyes!
'Cause we go together like ketchup and fries!"
With nose in the air and paws on the street,
Mr. Maple goes "Forward" and earns his first treat.
"Forward and left, then halt and go right!"
Mr. Maple relies on his laser-sharp sight.
Stepping in sync, oh what a dream!
"Hey, don't ya think we make a great team?"

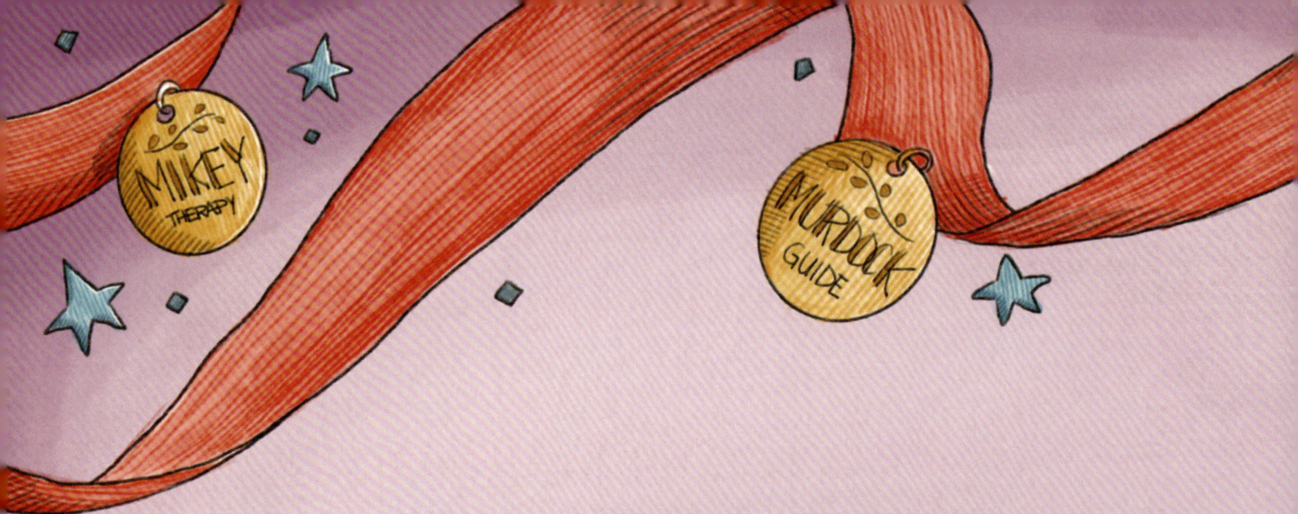

The whole of his life has led to this day.
This dog's on a mission, get out of his way!
He flew through the courses and rose to the top,
The crème de la crème, the cream of the crop!
Wear your cap proudly and put on your gown.
Look at you go, you're the talk of the town.
Sensational work, you should be proud.
"Mr. Maple, the Guide Dog!"
—say it out loud!

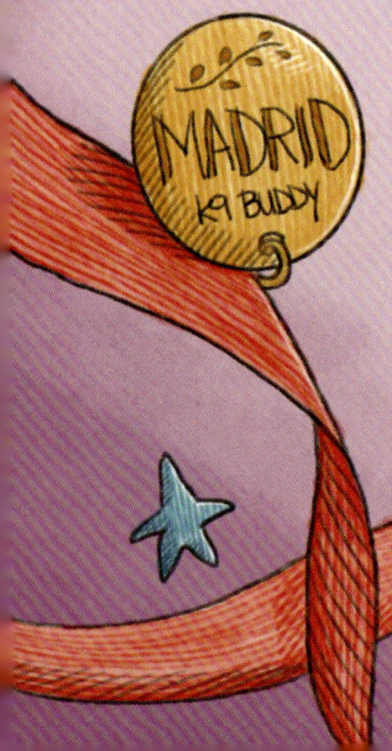

MASCOT
K9 BUDDY
MAJOR
THERAPY
MATRIX
PET
A+
MR MAPLE
GUIDE

Mr. Maple is ready to start his new role.
Guiding his person with heart and with soul.
“Not when he’s working” you’ll often hear said,
When somebody asks to pat his sweet head.
Together in stride, like a pod with two peas,
Walking with purpose and strolling with ease.
And as their bond deepens, let it be known:
When you’re a guide dog,
you’re never alone.

Guiding is great, but playtime is fun!
Unbuckle his harness, the workday is done!
When Maple is working, his name starts with Mister,
But when he's off-duty he's a fun-loving-twister!
Snugglin' and snoozin', zippin' and zoomin',
He's one lucky dog, and he loves his hooman!
He flops on his bed in a heap of pure bliss,
Rewarded each night with a cuddle and kiss.

ZOOM

As autumn leaves turn from greener to golder,
Guide dogs get wiser, and also get older.
Each passing season, new lessons are learned.
Love and Respect and Kibbles are earned!
From busy crosswalks to train station crowds,
He moves like a pro, both quiet and proud.
They've mastered the rhythm, the timing, the flow,
A magical pairing, wherever they go!

Mr. Maple takes charge in all kinds of weather,
"I've got your back, we're in this together!"
Through puddles and snowflakes, leading with grace,
Determined and steady, he sets the right pace.
No matter the season, no matter the skies,
Mr. Maple stays sharp and endlessly wise.
Storm clouds may gather, but never forget:
A guide dog still guides, even when wet!

M

Then at long last, the big day will come,
When working is over and guiding is done.
Stretch out on a beach or relax by a fire,
Mr. Maple, old boy! It's time to retire!
You may not be working, but still you will stay,
Right by your person at the end of each day.
And though your job's over, let it be known:
When you've been a guide dog,
you're never alone.

THE

END

Madrid: K9 Buddy

Major: Facility Dog

Matrix: Beloved Pet

Maple: Guide Dog

Murdock: Guide Dog

Marathon: Beloved Pet

Mikey: Facility Dog

Mascot: K9 Buddy

About the Author

Paul Castle is an author, illustrator, and social media content creator who believes every story should have a little heart, a little humor, and (if possible) at least one penguin. He lives in Seattle with his husband, Matthew, a classical violinist, and his guide dog, Mr. Maple, a very good boy with a very important job.

Born with Retinitis Pigmentosa, a degenerative eye disease, Paul has embraced creativity as both a passion and a way to navigate the world. As his vision has changed, he's adapted his artistic process using assistive technology, sheer determination, and Matthew's unending support. Whether sketching, painting, or bringing whimsical characters to life, Paul proves that storytelling has no limits, only new ways to be seen.

When they're not creating books, Paul and Matthew share their lives with millions online, making joyful, heartfelt content about love, blindness, and the occasional prank. Whether through stories, art, or adorable dog videos, Paul is always finding new ways to brighten the world, one page (or post) at a time.

Follow us @matthewandpaul
Visit PaulCastleStudio.com for more!

DOG DAY

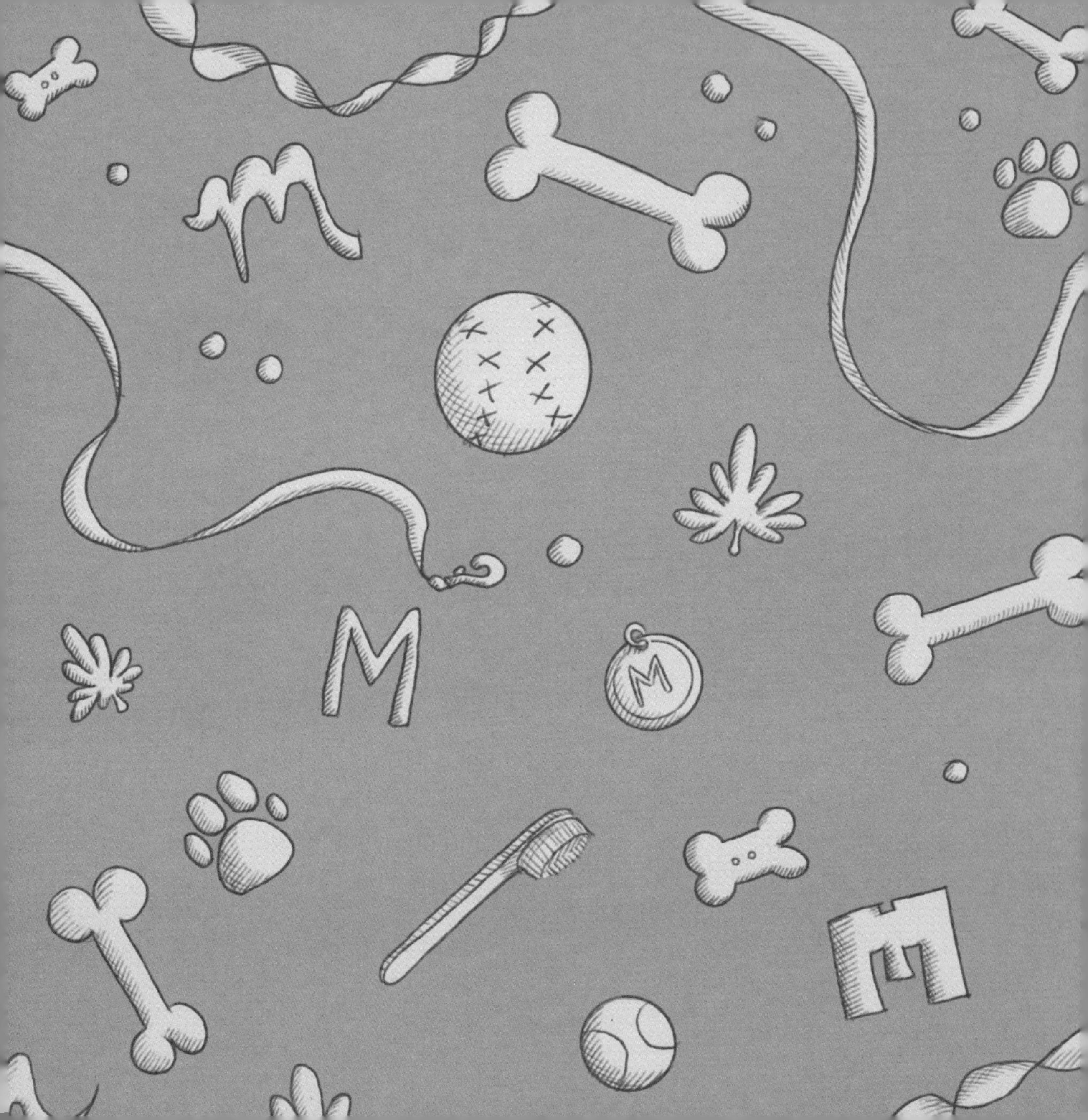